YOU Choose

Don't Get Angry, Annie

Stay Calm

Lisa Regan

It might be useful for parents or teachers to read our 'How to use this book' guide on pages 28–29 before looking at Annie's dilemmas. The points for discussion on these pages are helpful to share with your child once you have read the book together.

Published in paperback in 2014 by Wayland
Copyright © Wayland 2014

Wayland
338 Euston Road
London NW1 3BH

Wayland Australia
Level 17/207 Kent Street
Sydney, NSW 2000

Produced for Wayland by Calcium
Design: Paul Myerscough
Editor for Wayland: Victoria Brooker
Illustrations by Lucy Neale

British Library Cataloguing in Publication Data

Don't get angry, Annie. — (You choose)
    1. Anger—Juvenile literature. 2. Self-control—Juvenile
    literature.
    I. Series
    302.5'4–dc23

ISBN: 978 0 7502 8349 6

Printed in China

10 9 8 7 6 5 4 3 2 1

Wayland is a division of Hachette Children's Books,
an Hachette UK company.
www.hachette.co.uk

Contents

Hello, Annie!

Annie is **kind**. But sometimes she feels **angry**. When things don't work out quite right, Annie starts to feel really **cross**.

Follow Annie as she finds herself in tricky situations in which she must learn how to stay **calm**.

YOU

choose

too!

Play together, Annie

Annie's best friend, Rosie, is playing with Jamelia. Annie wishes Rosie was playing with her instead.

Annie can feel herself getting **cross**.

What should Annie choose to do?

Should Annie:

a push Jamelia away and play with Rosie instead?

b ask if she can play too?

c take all their toys away?

Annie, choose **b**

Friends shouldn't get cross if their friends play with other people. It's okay to have lots of different **playmates**. The important thing is to be nice so that they still want you as their friend, too.

What would YOU choose to do?

Don't spoil it, Annie

Annie is trying to draw a
dog, but she doesn't think
her drawing is very good.

Annie is getting **angry** with herself and with the picture.

What should Annie choose to do?

Should Annie:

a screw the paper into a ball and throw it across the room?

b scribble on it until she feels better?

c start a new drawing and try really hard to get it right?

Annie, choose **c**

You may not get everything right the very first time! Take a deep breath and try again. Your work will be better if you stay calm, rather than getting cross.

What would YOU choose to do?

Do as Mum says, Annie

Annie wants a cookie.
They look so yummy!

Her Mum says Annie can't have a cookie because it is almost time for her tea.

What should Annie choose to do?

Should Annie:

a go and play until tea is ready?

b **secretly** take a cookie when Mum isn't looking?

c get angry and shout that it's not fair?

Annie, choose **a**

Grown-ups usually have a good reason for saying no. Sometimes mums and dads do know best! Try to listen to them and do what they say, without getting angry.

What would YOU choose to do?

Be kind, Annie

Annie's little brother is **spoiling** her game. He's moving the pieces the wrong way.

Annie thinks he's too young to play properly.

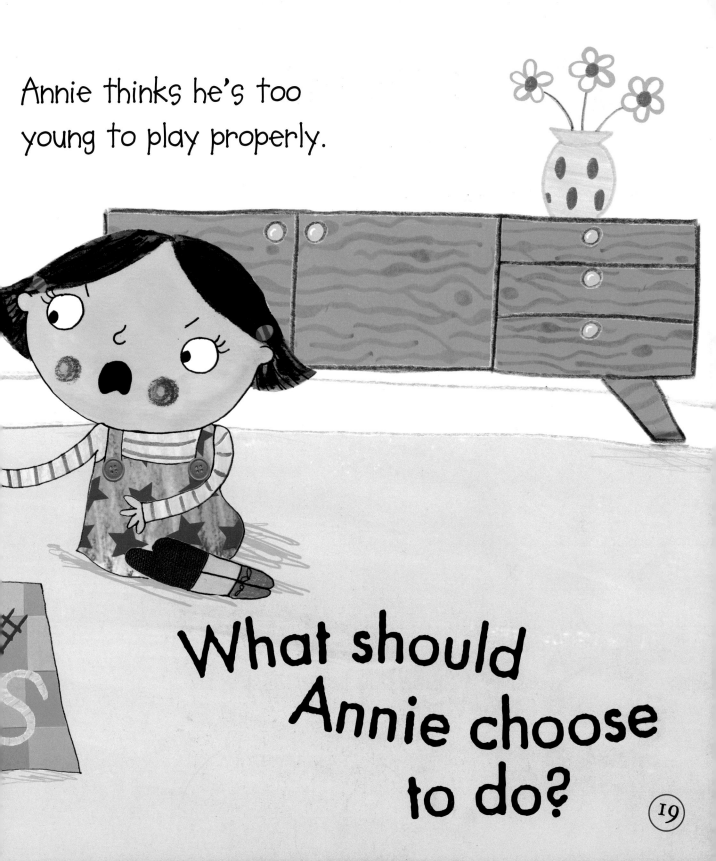

What should Annie choose to do?

Should Annie:

a scream at him that he ruins all her fun?

b push him over and run off to play in her room?

c make up an easier game so that her brother can join in?

Annie, choose **c**

When you were little, some things were hard for you, too. If you're feeling cross, count to 10 quietly. By then your anger should have started to go away.

What would **YOU** choose to do?

Stay calm, Annie

The teacher tells Annie off for talking in class.

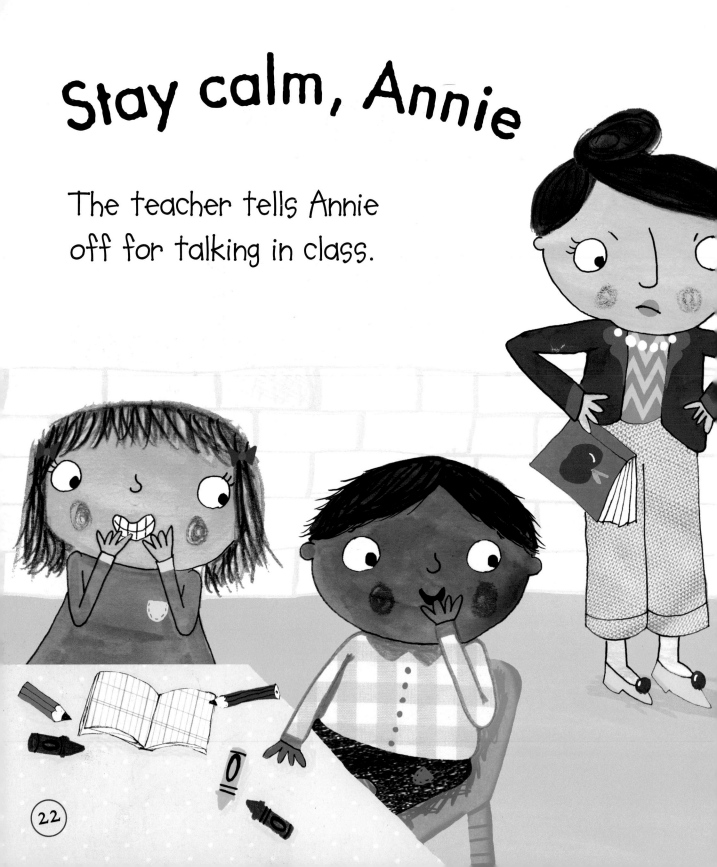

Annie feels so **angry** – she wasn't the only one talking!

What should Annie choose to do?

Should Annie:

a make a big **fuss** and shout in front of the whole class?

b pinch the other children who got her into trouble?

C stay quiet for the rest of the lesson so she doesn't get told off again?

Annie, choose **C**

It's hard to stay calm when you are told off for something that other people were doing wrong too. You can't change what has happened, but you can make sure you do the right thing next time.

What would YOU choose to do?

Well done, Annie!

Hey, look at Annie!
Now she can stay calm,
she's feeling much
happier.

Did you choose the right thing to do? If you did, big cheers for you!

If you chose some of the other answers, try to think about Annie's choices so you can stop yourself from getting cross next time. Then it will be big smiles all round!

And remember – don't get angry, stay calm!

How to use this book

This book can be used by a grown-up and a child together. It is based on common situations that pose a challenge to all children. Invite your child to talk about each of the choices. Ask questions such as 'Why do you think Annie should play with both Rosie and Jamelia?'.

Discuss the wrong choices, as well as the right ones, with your child. Describe what is happening in the following pictures and talk about what the wrong and right choices might be.

- Don't get cross because you're told not to do something. Adults have good reasons for their rules.

- It's okay to feel angry sometimes, but it isn't okay to take it out on others. Hurting people is wrong.

● Think about why other people do what they do, instead of getting angry with them.

● Don't destroy things if you feel angry. That will make you more cross!

Ask your child to imagine things that make them feel angry. Explain to them that it's okay to feel cross about some of these things. Tell them anger is a normal feeling for people to have, but let them know that they must learn to show their anger in a healthy way.

Talk about how showing anger by hitting or shouting can make people hurt others or spoil things. Show your child how they can express their anger in a healthy way, by telling others how they feel. Explain how good it feels to be in charge of the way you behave!

Glossary

calm not angry or cross

fuss bad behaviour such as shouting
   or complaining

kind to think about other people
   and their feelings

playmates friends to play with

properly in the right way, correctly

ruins spoiling something or breaking it

secretly doing or saying something
   in private, so no one else knows
   about what you are doing or saying

spoiling destroying something

Index

Titles in the series

ISBN: 978 0 7502 8349 6

Like all children, Annie sometimes gets really, really angry! She has lots of choices to make – but which are the CALM ones?

ISBN: 978 0 7502 6724 3

Like all children, Carlos sometimes does things that are wrong, and doesn't come clean. He has lots of choices to make – but which are the TRUTHFUL ones?

ISBN: 978 0 7502 6722 9

Like all children, Charlie sometimes feels a little scared. He has lots of choices to make – but which are the BRAVE ones?

ISBN: 978 0 7502 6725 0

Like all children, Gertie sometimes plays a little dirty. We put Gertie on the spot with some tricky problems and ask her to decide what is FAIR!

ISBN: 978 0 7502 6723 6

Like all children, Harry sometimes takes things that don't belong to him. He has lots of choices to make – but which are the HONEST ones?

ISBN: 978 0 7502 8344 1

Like all children, Henry sometimes gets angry and sometimes he hits, too. He has lots of choices to make – but which are the GENTLE ones?

ISBN: 978 0 7502 8350 2

Like all children, Sam sometimes feels sad, and he doesn't know how to make himself feel better. He has lots of choices to make – but which are the HAPPY ones?

ISBN: 978 0 7502 8343 4

Like all children, Tilly wants to do everything *right now*, and sometimes she just can't wait! She has lots of choices to make – but which are the PATIENT ones?